KT-416-974

Skulduggery Pleasant
THE END OF THE WORLD

This book has been specially written and published for World Book Day 2012. For further information please see www.worldbookday.com

World Book Day in the UK and Ireland is made possible by generous sponsorship from National Book Tokens, participating publishers, authors and booksellers. Booksellers who accept the £1 World Book Day Token bear the full cost of redeeming it.

Also by Derek Landy:

DEREK LANDY

Skulduggery Pleasant
THE END OF THE WORLD

HarperCollins *Children's Books*

First published in paperback in Great Britain for World Book Day
by HarperCollins *Children's Books* 2012
HarperCollins *Children's Books* is a division of
HarperCollins*Publishers* Ltd
77-85 Fulham Palace Road, Hammersmith, London W6 8JB

Visit us on the web at www.harpercollins.co.uk

Visit Skulduggery Pleasant online at
www.skulduggerypleasant.co.uk

Derek Landy blogs under duress at
www.dereklandy.blogspot.com

1

Illuminated letters © Tom Percival 2012
Skulduggery Pleasant™ Derek Landy
SP Logo™ HarperCollins Publishers

ISBN 978-0-00-745820-2

Printed and bound in England by
Clays Ltd, St Ives plc

This book is dedicated to cover artist
extraordinaire, Tom Percival.

For most people, the cover is the reason they pick up
a book in the first place. The amount of correspondence
I get proves this, as people go on and on about how the cover
caught their eye, made them want to read about a skeleton
detective, how the covers are the best things ever,
how the covers blah blah blah…

I think it's a generally agreed upon fact that I could draw the
covers if I really wanted to. I have the raw talent, I have the eye,
and I have that one year of art college under my belt.

And I think Tom knows this, which is why he pushes himself to
excel each and every time, why he pushes himself to make these
books stand out from the others on the shelf. The threat I pose
is important. The threat I pose is a good motivator.

Keep pushing yourself, Tom. My time is coming.

P.S. You're welcome.

ONE

The man with the unfortunate face stood in the aisle between the Science Fiction section and Crime, and he seemed to be trying to blend in with the bookshelves. He wasn't doing a particularly good job of it. When an old woman shuffled too close, he snarled at her – actually *snarled* – and the old woman yelped like an injured puppy and hurried away as fast as her little old legs would carry her. People weren't used to snarling, not in a public library. For as long as he'd been coming here, Ryan certainly hadn't witnessed any snarling. Until today, of course.

He watched the man out of the corner of his eye, watched him whispering with his companions. They were an odd bunch. The snarling man was the biggest – arms like tree trunks, black matted hair completely failing to hide a face that was in no way attractive.

The smallest one of the group was a middle-aged man who stood very still and didn't join in with the whispering. He looked like an accountant who'd wandered out of the office one day and had accidentally joined a biker gang. The woman beside him wore battered leather and had short spiky hair. She was pretty, in a sinister sort of way, but she didn't have a very nice laugh. It carried through the quiet building, unnerving all who heard it. The librarians, usually so strict about things like that, pretended not to notice.

The final member of the gang seemed to be the leader. He was lean and his arms looked strong. He had tattoos curling down from beneath his T-shirt. His jeans were black and his boots were scuffed.

He had dark hair that hung over his brow. The big man and the woman would whisper to him and he'd nod. He never stopped looking around, though. Once or twice he almost caught Ryan's eye.

Ryan sat back in his chair, exited his email account on the computer. No emails. As usual. No one ever sent him emails. Not even spam. Maybe if he made more friends, like his mother was always saying, maybe then he'd at least be sent some junk every once in a while. Fifteen years old and no friends. It was kind of sad, when he thought about it. He didn't think about it much.

He got up, walked through the Children's section, running his fingers along the spines of the books he passed. He found himself in History and picked a book at random. Something about the Second World War. He didn't care. He was just here to waste time, after all – waste time and build up the courage to run away.

It wasn't his mother's fault. It wasn't even his new stepdad's fault. Ryan didn't have a problem with either of them. He just missed his father so much, and every moment spent living in that house reminded him that his father was dead and gone and never coming back, and Ryan didn't want to live like that any more. So he was going to run away to... somewhere. Somewhere else. Just for a little while. Just to get away.

He put the book back and went to take another one, but something fell from the shelf. He saw a flash of silver – what looked like a clasp, or a brooch – and without thinking he reached out and caught it, closed his fingers round it tight. It was cold to the touch, but immediately turned hot. Pain lanced up his arm and he cried out. He opened his hand to drop it, but the only thing he was holding was silver dust. The clasp, whatever it was, had crumbled away in his grip.

The pain was gone too. Not wanting to make a mess, Ryan emptied the silver dust on to a gap in the bookshelf, then brushed at his hand. There was something smudged on his palm. He tried to wipe it away, but it wouldn't come off. Then he realised his skin wasn't smudged – it was burned. The clasp had burned itself into his flesh.

"What you got there?"

Ryan turned at the sound of the voice. It was the leader of the gang. The other three stood behind him. They were all looking at him like he was prey.

"Nothing," Ryan mumbled, closing his hand.

"We heard you cry out," said the man. "We heard you cry out and Mercy said – that's Mercy over there – Mercy said let's see if he needs any help."

"I said that," the woman with the spiky hair confirmed, nodding her spiky head. "I was worried. Because I care."

"She does care," said the leader. "She wanted to know if you'd hurt yourself. Have you hurt yourself? She wanted to know if you'd hurt yourself and Obloquy said – Obloquy's the big lad – Obloquy said how is he going to hurt himself in a library? Is he going to paper-cut himself to death?"

The leader laughed, and Mercy laughed, and the big one grinned.

"I'm funny," he said.

"How did you hurt yourself?" the leader asked, coming down off the laugh with a friendly chuckle.

"I didn't hurt myself," said Ryan. "I'm fine."

"But we heard you cry out," said the man, suddenly frowning. "We heard you. Didn't we hear him?"

"I heard him," said Mercy.

"I heard him too, Foe," said Obloquy.

The middle-aged man, the accountant, didn't say anything.

The leader, Foe, examined Ryan curiously. "You don't have to be scared of us. Is that what's wrong? You're scared of us? You don't have to be. We're not bad people."

Obloquy laughed, and Mercy jammed an elbow into his ribs to shut him up.

"I know you're not supposed to talk to strangers," Foe continued, "but aren't you a bit old for that? Isn't that rule more for kids? You're not a kid any more, are you? What are you, fifteen or so?" He reached out, dipping a finger into the silver dust on the bookshelf, then bringing it to the tip of his tongue. He tasted it, and smiled at Ryan. "And if you don't talk to strangers, how are you going to make friends? Friends are important. We want to be friends."

"We really do," said Mercy.

"And we were standing over there," said Foe, "talking about books, because that's what we like to do, we like to talk about books, and we heard you cry out and we came over because we were worried, and we care, and now we're here, having a conversation. Having a friendly conversation with our new friend."

"I didn't hurt myself," Ryan said, really wishing he were somewhere else right now.

"Friends don't lie to each other," Foe said.

"I'm – I'm not lying."

"You're lying a little bit," Foe said, smiling. "What's your name?"

"Ryan."

"Good to meet you, Ryan."

Foe stuck out his hand. Ryan hesitated, then went to shake it. Instead, Foe grabbed his wrist and turned his palm to face upwards. The gang looked at the symbol imprinted on to his skin, and Foe released Ryan's wrist and put his hand on Ryan's shoulder. "Ryan, my friend. You're going to have to come with us now."

Ryan shook his head. "I should be going home. My dad will be here in a minute to pick me up."

"Ryan," said Foe. "If you don't come with us right this second, we're going to kill everyone in this building and then we're going to drag you out through the blood and the gore and what remains of their dead bodies." Another smile, this time with narrowed eyes. "So really, buddy, it's up to you."

Ryan wanted to scream for help and run away, but his legs wouldn't work and his chest was too tight. He looked at them. Foe, with his smile and his eyes. Mercy, an eager look on her face, like she was really hoping she'd get to kill someone today. Obloquy, standing there looking dumb and dangerous. And the accountant, whose gaze had never faltered, who was as still as a statue, completely detached from what was going on. The accountant was the scariest of them all.

And then, whistling.

TWO

Through the gaps in the books, Ryan could see someone in the next aisle over, moving slowly. Someone in black. Someone whistling. Ryan recognised the tune. It was the theme music to *Harry Potter*.

A pretty girl appeared at the corner of the bookcase. Tall, with long dark hair. Maybe a year or two older than Ryan. Wearing a jacket that was zipped up, tight trousers and boots, and a ring on her finger. All in black. All made from materials Ryan couldn't identify.

And still, whistling. As she whistled, her dark eyes wandered from Ryan to Foe, to Mercy and Obloquy, and then to the accountant. When she got to the accountant, she stopped whistling, and looked back at Ryan.

"Hi," she said. "My name's Valkyrie. Are these people bothering you?"

Ryan wanted to tell her to run, but he knew the gang would be on her in an instant.

The girl looked at Foe. "I'm part of Library Security," she said. "We've had some reports of overdue books in this area, and I'm going to need to ask you all some questions. We can do this here or downtown – where we'd actually have more space and access to a coffee machine."

Something was wrong. Foe didn't threaten her and Mercy didn't say anything at all. In fact, Mercy and Obloquy were glancing around, like they expected someone else to show up. Even the accountant looked wary.

"You really want this to happen?" Foe asked, his voice low. "Here? In a public place? Where all these innocent people might get caught in the crossfire?"

The pretty girl, Valkyrie, gave him a shrug. "I'm just looking for a way to spoil your day, Vincent. The choice is yours. Stick around and get beaten up and thrown in a cell, or leave, now. Immediately."

"Sure," said Foe. "We'll just take Ryan here with us."

Valkyrie shook her head. "Ryan stays, I'm afraid."

"Ah. Well, see, now we have a problem."

"That's too bad."

"That's just what I was thinking."

Valkyrie moved, snapping her palm against the air and the air shimmered and Foe shot back off his feet, colliding with Mercy. Before Ryan could even wonder what had just happened, she grabbed him and then they were running through the aisles. A stream of red energy sizzled by his ear and Ryan shrieked, tried to throw himself to the ground but Valkyrie wouldn't let him.

"Keep moving," she snapped.

He stumbled after her.

There was a roar, and the crash of a bookcase being toppled. Ryan glanced back, saw Obloquy go hurtling through the air, and a man stepped into view – a tall man, thin, wearing a dark blue suit and hat, like one of those old-fashioned private eyes.

Another stream of red energy burst through the bookshelf to his left and Ryan forgot all about the thin man and focused all his attention on not dying. Mercy smashed into him and he went sprawling across the floor, the wind knocked out of him. Then Valkyrie was there, running straight for Mercy who turned to her, opened her mouth wide, and let loose another stream of energy. From her mouth. *From her mouth.*

Ryan blinked.

Valkyrie dived, rolled, came up and threw herself into Mercy. Mercy grunted, the stream cut off, and they went down. They grappled, throwing elbows and pulling hair. Mercy grabbed a handful of Valkyrie's hair and yanked and Valkyrie slammed her forehead into Mercy's face. Mercy screamed with pain and rage and Valkyrie was on top now,

Mercy trying to push her off. Valkyrie trapped one of Mercy's arms and moved up, too fast for Ryan to work out what was happening, but somehow she swung her leg over Mercy and was now leaning back sharply. She snapped Mercy's elbow and Mercy howled, and then Valkyrie was scrambling towards Ryan, pulling him to his feet.

Ryan wished he could have said something intelligent to her at that moment, but all he could manage was "Muh". It was not very impressive.

Around them, the good people of the library cowered behind cover or ran for the exits. Ryan would have given anything to be allowed to cower. His entire body ached to find a dark corner and collapse into it like some kind of jelly. But the pretty girl who was gripping his hand kept pulling him on through the stacks, and Ryan was suddenly determined not to embarrass himself in front of her. So he forced his legs to stay strong and when Valkyrie hesitated, he overtook her.

"This way," he said, and now he was pulling her through the stacks, and she was probably thinking what a great guy he was, and look how take-charge he is, and even though he's a year or two younger than I am he'd probably make a great boyfriend and when all this is over, I'll probably want to kiss him or something. Ryan nodded to himself. Yeah, she was probably thinking all that as he led her through the aisles and the stacks, and then they came to a wall with a nice picture on it.

"Moron," Valkyrie snapped, turning and yanking him after her.

"Sorry," he said.

"I thought you knew where you were going!"

"I thought there was a door here."

She stopped suddenly and he ran into the back of her. He was halfway through apologising when he saw the accountant standing ahead of them.

Elsewhere in the library, the thin man was still battling the others. There were a lot of crashes and yells and screams and grunts. But here, with Ryan and Valkyrie and the accountant, it somehow seemed really, really quiet.

The accountant took a step forward. Valkyrie

took a step back. She stepped on Ryan's foot and he said "Ow" and then apologised. She didn't hear him.

She snapped her hand against the air. The space rippled and a bookcase was blasted back, but the accountant was already moving. Then Valkyrie clicked her fingers and Ryan yelped when fire suddenly flared in her palm. He tore off his jacket and flung it over her forearm, batting out the flames.

"What the hell are you doing?" she raged, trying to push him back.

"You're on fire!" he squealed manfully.

She pulled away from him, her hand still ablaze, and then she flung the fire, but the accountant twisted, impossibly fast, and the fireball missed him, exploded against the side of another bookcase. The accountant darted out of sight.

"Oh," Ryan said.

Valkyrie backed up against him. "If you see an exit," she whispered, "you run to it. Understand?"

He nodded.

Something moved above them and the

accountant dropped down on to Valkyrie. She cried out and Ryan stumbled back, watched as the accountant grabbed her and threw her like she was nothing. Valkyrie disappeared among the stacks.

Ryan spun, and ran. He didn't know where he was going, but anywhere was better than where he'd just been. The accountant was following, but he had leaped back up so he was off the ground, gliding from bookcase to bookcase, like a hawk chasing a terrified field mouse.

Then Ryan saw it – a green EXIT sign over a fire door. He changed direction, almost tripped over a cowering man who was hiding in the Reference section, and ran on. He was almost at the door when he glanced back over his shoulder, saw the accountant leaping for him. Valkyrie emerged from the stacks and something was happening to her right hand – it was covered in writhing, moving shadows. She whipped her hand and a trail of darkness reached for the accountant, wrapped around his leg. Valkyrie pulled back, hard, and the accountant crunched to the ground.

He snarled, sprang up and turned, and Valkyrie sent a wave of shadows crashing into him. He hit the far wall and that's all Ryan saw, because Valkyrie was pushing him out through the fire door. The alarm wailed as they emerged into the narrow alley behind the library. With Valkyrie's hand pressing into his back, Ryan sprinted towards the road. A gleaming black car was parked illegally, like it was waiting for them. It looked old, but a brand-new kind of old.

Valkyrie opened the door, bundled him in the back. She got in behind the wheel, leaving the door open. She started the car and the engine roared, and she slipped into the passenger seat and buckled her belt.

"Seatbelt," she ordered.

Ryan buckled his seatbelt. He looked at the empty driver's seat. "Does it drive itself?" he asked.

"Don't be thick," she replied, looking back at the library. "He just hates it when I drive the Bentley, that's all."

The thin man came sprinting out of the library,

clutching his hat in one gloved hand. Ryan blinked. The way the sun caught his bald head made it seem almost white, almost like...

Ryan swallowed. It wasn't the sun. The thin man wasn't bald.

The thin man was a skeleton.

Ryan screamed as the skeleton jumped in behind the wheel.

"Shut him up, please," the skeleton said as the car shot forward.

"Shut up, Ryan," said Valkyrie.

Foe came charging out of the library but the car, the Bentley, was already slicing through traffic. And still Ryan screamed.

"Ryan," Valkyrie said, "stop that."

"He's a skeleton!" Ryan yelled. "Look at him! They killed your friend!"

"No they didn't," said the skeleton. "But they punched me. A lot. And one of them hit me with a desk. Have you ever been hit with a desk, Ryan? It's sore."

"I was hit with a desk once," Valkyrie said.

"Oh, that's right," said the skeleton. "It really hurts, doesn't it?"

"It does."

Ryan sat in the back seat, petrified. Valkyrie turned to him, sighed, and then gave him the kind of smile usually reserved for idiots, or toddlers, or idiot toddlers.

"Hi," she said. "I'm Valkyrie Cain. My partner here is Skulduggery Pleasant. We just saved your life. The least you can do is not throw up in our car."

THREE

The skeleton's jaw moved when he talked, but he had no tongue. He had no lungs, or vocal cords. There was nothing at all to give him a voice, and yet Skulduggery still talked. Good God, did he talk.

"The short version," he said as they drove, "is that magic exists. Monsters exist. Sorcerers, like myself and Valkyrie, fight to stop other sorcerers, like Foe and his friends, from doing bad things. We're the heroes, if you really must give us a title. They're the villains. We try to stay out of the public eye as much as possible. It's really quite straightforward if you don't think about it too hard."

"But I don't understand," Ryan whispered.

"That's the spirit," Skulduggery said. "We don't have an awful lot of time, so there are some things you're just going to have to accept."

"You're a skeleton."

"Like that."

"But how can you move?"

Valkyrie undid her seatbelt and climbed into the back. "Ryan," she said when she was settled, "the world is an amazing place. It's full of wonderful things and fascinating people and deep mysteries just waiting to be uncovered. In order to not annoy me, though, you've really got to put all of that to one side and concentrate on what we tell you. He's a walking skeleton. I wear tight trousers. Do you have any questions so far?"

"Uh, no."

"Excellent."

"You can feel safe with us," Skulduggery said. "We've saved the world a few times and we've become quite good at it. Really, if I were you, there's no one else I'd rather be with at a time like this."

"Skulduggery," Valkyrie said, "your façade."

"Oh, yes," he said, and his gloved fingers tapped his collarbones. A face flowed up, covering his skull with skin and hair and features. He smiled at a lady in a car they passed and she frowned at him.

"He can only wear a face for half an hour every day," Valkyrie whispered to Ryan. "So he tends to overdo it on the sociable front."

"But all that went on in a library," Ryan said, finally confident enough to form a complete sentence without gibbering. "It's going to be all over the news."

"Actually," Valkyrie responded, "it's not. We have people for that sort of thing. Sometime within the next hour a very nice man called Geoffrey is going to convince everyone who witnessed that fight that they didn't see what they thought they saw. He's kind of a Public Relations officer, in a way – making sure the civilian world doesn't notice the rest of us as we go about our business."

Skulduggery glanced at Ryan over his shoulder. The face he wore was dark-haired and sallow-skinned. "Some people, like Geoffrey, find they are suited to non-combative roles. He's what we call a Sensitive – someone with psychic abilities. Some Sensitives read minds, some see the future – Geoffrey just makes you believe whatever he tells you. Another Sensitive was a man called Deacon Maybury. Which is where you come in."

"I've never heard of him," Ryan said.

"Of course not," said Valkyrie. "I hadn't either, up until a few days ago. I'd heard of his brother, Davit, who died. There were sextuplets, apparently. Six identical Mayburys. Only four now, though."

"This Deacon Maybury, he's dead too?"

Skulduggery turned the Bentley off the busy road, down a quieter street. "Deacon was a Sensitive who worked for the Sanctuary – where we work. Sometimes we arrest criminals for whom there is no redemption. If they're susceptible, it's possible to enter their mind and insert a new personality. It's always been a controversial procedure, and it only works if the criminal's will is weak, but the old personality would be subdued, the new one would have a life and a history and memories, and the criminal would get a chance at a normal life. Inserting new personalities was Deacon's job."

"But he got bored," Valkyrie said. "We spoke to people who knew him. He wanted adventure and excitement. He wanted money and power. So he fell in with the wrong crowd – Foe and his gang."

Skulduggery nodded. "A very bad lot. Vincent Foe was a mercenary during the war. I won't tell you what war, I don't want to complicate things. Mercy Charient is, for all intents and purposes, a serial killer. Obloquy, I doubt you'll disagree, is something of a moron – but a savage moron. And then there's Samuel."

Valkyrie made a face. "Bloody vampires."

Ryan sat forward. "That was a vampire? That guy who looked like an accountant?"

"We don't talk about vampires," Skulduggery warned.

"But it was daytime. How could he have been

out during the—"

"We don't talk about vampires!" Valkyrie said sharply.

Ryan shrank back. "Sorry," he said.

"Don't worry about it," Skulduggery told him. "Valkyrie used to date a vampire, that's all."

"We didn't *date*," Valkyrie said immediately.

Skulduggery held a hand up. "I'm not judging."

Valkyrie scowled, and looked back at Ryan. "Anyway, Deacon Maybury fell in with Foe's gang, and Foe's gang are nuts. Some people want to take over the world. Some people want to change the world. Foe and his mates want to destroy the world." She shook her head. "They're idiots."

"Nihilists," Skulduggery corrected.

"Idiots," Valkyrie repeated. "There's something called a Doomsday Machine, Ryan. Yes, I know how that sounds. And yes, it is as stupid as it appears. Some genius went ahead and built a bomb that could blow up the planet. He said he built it so that if the Faceless Ones ever returned, we could kill ourselves and kill them at the same time so that they could never travel to and infect other realities."

Ryan frowned. "Faceless Ones?"

"Don't complicate things," Skulduggery said.

"Yeah, sorry Ryan," said Valkyrie. "Anyway, that's why it exists. So it was sitting there, existing, not harming anyone, and then a few years ago it was stolen. Foe and his gang stole it and hid it – which wouldn't be an easy thing to do because the Machine is bigger than a house."

"Why did they hide it?" Ryan asked. "Why not just set if off?"

"Because they didn't have the key," Skulduggery said. "They spent the next few years searching for it. That's when Deacon joined them. They finally found it, nine days ago. But Deacon had no intention of activating the Machine. He hid the key, shaped like a clasp, to sell to the highest bidder."

"But Foe's gang caught up with him before the auction could take place," Valkyrie said. "They chased him and he accidentally fell into a wood chipper."

Ryan winced.

"Yeah," said Valkyrie.

"So now Foe is hunting for the key," Skulduggery said. "Their hunt led them to the library, and our hunt led us to them. And both hunts have led to you, Ryan."

Ryan looked at his hand. "But the key's gone. It crumbled when I held it. It's just dust now."

"The key wasn't what you held," Skulduggery said. "It's the imprint it left on your skin. I've got good news and bad news for you, Ryan. The bad news is that you're the only one in the world who can activate the Doomsday Machine, and Foe and his gang are never going to stop coming after you. The good news is that with myself and Valkyrie protecting you, you stand a very good chance of emerging from this relatively unscathed."

Valkyrie looked at the back of Skulduggery's head. "You said they'd probably try to cut his hand off."

"I said relatively," Skulduggery reminded her.

FOUR

Deacon Maybury's apartment was trashed.

Skulduggery and Valkyrie went first, to check if it was safe, and Ryan crept in after them. Papers littered the bad carpet. The ugly couch had been slashed open and its stuffing had been pulled out like fluffy intestines. Chairs were overturned, picture frames smashed and every drawer taken from its slot, the contents dumped and scattered.

"What exactly are we looking for in this

mess?" Valkyrie asked.

"Foe secured the Doomsday Machine somewhere," Skulduggery said, picking through the debris. "We need to find out where. Maybe we'll get lucky and discover that Deacon was an avid journal keeper. But if we can't find a solid lead to take us to the Machine, there might be something else here, a clue or a name, something that will take us a step further."

Valkyrie sighed. "I hate looking for clues."

Ryan smiled at the cuteness of Valkyrie's sulk.

"Looking for clues is an integral part of detective work," Skulduggery told her.

"I prefer the part where we hit people."

"That's just because you have a violent nature. You should endeavour to be more peace-loving, like Ryan."

Ryan stopped admiring Valkyrie and frowned. "Why am I peace-loving?"

"Hmm?" Skulduggery said, looking up. "Oh, I meant nothing by it. I just assumed you were peace-loving because you seem to be terrible at violence. Plus, you scream a lot."

"Just because I don't go around getting into fights every day doesn't mean I can't fight," Ryan said, his face growing warm.

"Not being good at violence is nothing to be ashamed of," Skulduggery said, standing a filing cabinet upright and sifting through it. "If there were more people like you in the world, there'd be less need for people like us."

"I don't have a violent nature," Valkyrie growled.

"And I'm not peace-loving," Ryan insisted.

"But you do scream a lot," Skulduggery said.

"How can you know that?" Ryan asked. "You've known me for, like, two hours."

"And in those two hours, you have spent most of your time screaming." Skulduggery shrugged. "I really can't see how my logic can be faulted."

"I don't have a violent nature," Valkyrie repeated.

"Of course you don't," Skulduggery said, as he continued to sift the files in the cabinet. "Entirely my mistake."

Valkyrie scowled and started sorting through the

papers on the floor. She hadn't been too interested in Ryan's defence of his manliness. He couldn't say he blamed her. She was a sorcerer who battled evil villains every other day. He was a chubby loser who needed girls to fight his battles for him. The only way he was going to change how she thought of him was to do something so brave and noble that she couldn't fail to be impressed. He turned and screamed at a middle-aged woman who stood in the doorway.

The middle-aged woman was startled by the scream, but not half as startled as Ryan himself. It had been a surprisingly high-pitched scream this time, and to make matters worse, it resulted in Valkyrie leaping in front of him protectively.

"Oh," said the middle-aged woman. She wore a floral dress and a cardigan. As middle-aged women went, she wasn't particularly frightening.

Skulduggery walked forward, a new false face smiling broadly. "Hello there," he said. "How are you on this fine day? Come in, come in. And you are...?"

"Francine," the woman said, a little flustered. "I live down the hall... What are you doing in Deacon Maybury's apartment?"

"You know Deacon?" Skulduggery asked. Valkyrie walked behind her, checked the corridor for anyone else, then stepped back in and closed the door.

"Well, yes," said Francine, frowning at Valkyrie and then looking at Skulduggery. "He's my neighbour and he's a good man. If you're robbing him, I must warn you – we don't take kindly to that sort of thing here."

"We're not robbing him," Skulduggery said. "But I'm afraid I have some bad news."

"Is it Deacon?" Francine asked, her eyes wide.

"It is."

"Is he sick?"

"It's a little worse than that."

She gasped. "He's dying?"

"He was briefly dying," said Skulduggery. "Now he's dead."

Francine's mouth dropped open. "What?

Deacon... Deacon is *dead*?"

"I'm afraid so."

"Oh no. Oh no, no, no." She sagged, and Valkyrie caught her before she collapsed. "My Deacon... My poor Deacon..."

Valkyrie staggered over to the only upright chair, and dumped Francine into it.

"He was so strong," Francine sobbed. "So proud. So much dignity. How did he die?"

"Wood chipper," said Valkyrie.

Francine wailed again, pounding the table with her little fists. "Why?" she cried. "Why did you take him, Lord?"

Valkyrie looked at Skulduggery, and Skulduggery shrugged.

"Uh," Valkyrie said. "I'm sorry for your, you know, your loss. I'm sure he was a great... I'm sure..." She faltered, and gave a shrug of her own. Ryan looked at Skulduggery, but he showed no signs of offering any real comfort to the poor woman.

"You obviously loved him very much," Ryan said, surprising himself by stepping forward.

"I did," Francine sobbed.

"I'm sure he loved you back."

Francine looked up, her eyes red and puffy and pleading. "Did he ever mention me?"

Ryan hesitated, and Valkyrie smirked at him from behind Francine. "All the time," he said. "Yes. God, every time I spoke to him he was all, Francine this and Francine that and... ohh, how I love Francine."

"He said that?"

"Uh, something along those lines, definitely..."

Francine clasped her hands to her chest. "I knew it," she said. "I knew he loved me. All those long silences. All those awkward moments. I should have told him I felt the same way. Then we could have... Then we could have..."

She broke off into a fit of sobbing. Behind her, Valkyrie gave Ryan the thumbs up. He had a feeling she meant it sarcastically.

"Did you talk to Deacon much?" Skulduggery asked, leaning down to gently pat her hand. "Did you tell each other about your days? Did you confide in each other...?"

"With a love like ours," Francine warbled, "we didn't need words."

"How inconvenient," Skulduggery muttered, straightening up immediately and walking away.

"Francine," Ryan said, "we're looking for something that Deacon was keeping for us. Do you know where it is? It'd be big, now, as big as a house."

Francine blinked away tears. "What could he have had that was as big as a house?"

Ryan frowned. He really had no answer to that.

"A house," Valkyrie said quickly. "He had a house. He was keeping it for us. One of those mobile houses, you know the kind."

"A mobile home?" Francine asked.

"Something like that. A little bigger. Do you remember if he ever mentioned a warehouse, or some kind of big storage facility that he visited?"

Francine frowned. "Well, I... I heard him on the phone once. I remember him saying something about having the paperwork for a warehouse that was cluttering up his files."

"It has to be here somewhere," Skulduggery

said, going back to the filing cabinet. Valkyrie went into the bedroom, started pulling the place apart.

"Did I say something wrong?" Francine asked.

"No," Ryan said. "Actually, you've been a big help. Would you like something? A cup of tea or...?"

"I should get back to my apartment," Francine said, standing slowly. "I need a lie-down. This is all... this is all a big shock to me."

"I'm really sorry," Ryan said.

She smiled weakly, took a step and swayed. Ryan jumped for her, wrapping one of her arms round his neck.

"I'll help you," he said.

"Thank you," she replied. A tear rolled down her cheek. "You're very nice."

While Skulduggery and Valkyrie searched, Ryan hobbled along with Francine out of the apartment and down the corridor. She was light but awkward.

"Your friends are a little odd," Francine said.

"I know."

"The girl's pretty, though. Is she your girlfriend?"

Ryan gave a laugh, realised he was blushing.

"No, she's not. We've just met, actually."

"My apartment's around the corner," Francine said, gesturing ahead of them and sniffling. "Do you want my advice? Don't make the same mistake I made with Deacon. Tell her how you feel."

"I really just met her."

"But you like her, don't you?"

"I, yeah, I suppose."

He helped her round the corner.

"Seize the moment," Francine said. "You never know when you might get another chance at happiness."

"I'll think about it," he promised, hoping that she'd change the subject before anyone overheard them.

"My apartment's just up ahead," Francine said, standing a little straighter. "You really are very nice. Such good manners, helping me all the way to my door."

"It's no trouble at all."

"Unfortunately," Francine said, "it will be."

"Sorry? It will be what?"

"Trouble," Francine said. "It will be a lot of trouble."

Vincent Foe walked out of the apartment ahead of them.

FIVE

Ryan spun, grabbed Francine, tried to drag her with him, but she laughed. She got an arm round his throat before he could call for help and hauled him backwards. He kicked and struggled, but she was much too strong, and then he was in the apartment and Foe was closing the door behind them.

Francine released him, and Ryan jumped away, almost colliding with Obloquy. Samuel watched him from the corner of the room.

"If you shout or scream," Foe said, "we'll kill you."

"And then we'll kill Valkyrie," said Francine. She looked at Foe, and grinned. "He's got a little crush on her."

Foe raised an eyebrow. "Is that right? Well, can't say I blame you, Ryan – she is a fine-looking girl. If I were a few hundred years younger, I'd be in there like a shot, believe you me. I'm not altogether sure what she'd ever see in *you*, though. You don't seem quite up to her standard. No offence, but you're kind of... unexceptional."

"Maybe he's hoping she'll like him for his sense of humour," Obloquy chuckled.

"Young love," Foe said, almost wistfully. "If you're lucky, you might have a chance to confess to her your eternal devotion, so long as you do exactly what I tell you."

Ryan's mouth was so dry his voice was a croak. "I'm not going to help you destroy the world."

"Yes you are."

"It doesn't make any sense. If you want to die, why don't you just kill yourselves and leave everyone else out of it?"

"Where's the drama in that?" asked Francine.

Foe glanced at her. "That's getting really disconcerting, you know."

"Ain't that something?" she murmured, and Ryan watched as Francine flickered, and he glimpsed someone underneath, someone slimmer, wearing black, with a bandaged arm... And then Francine was gone, and Mercy stood there. "That better?"

"Much," Foe said, turning his attention back to Ryan. "We're going to destroy the world because there is absolutely no point to its continued existence."

There were a hundred things Ryan wanted to say. *That's it? That's the reason? You want to kill everyone because you can't see the point? What kind of stupid, pathetic, selfish reason is that?* But he didn't say any of it, because he was too scared. Because he wasn't the hero. Because he was the one who was waiting for someone to rescue him.

There was a knock on the door.

"Francine?"

It was Valkyrie's voice. Mercy stepped up to

Ryan, pressing a blade against his belly.

"Francine," Valkyrie called, "is Ryan in there with you?"

Foe looked at Ryan, and held his finger to his lips as Obloquy went to the door. The knife dug into Ryan's skin painfully. He had to warn her. He had to. He couldn't just stand here and keep quiet.

"I know what you're thinking," Mercy whispered. "I can see it all over your face. Just know that if you make a sound, I'll kill you and cut off your hand."

Valkyrie knocked again, and Mercy looked towards the door, and a sudden pressure built up inside Ryan until he shoved her away from him. And then Samuel was there, a hand closing round his throat and Ryan was moving with his feet off the ground, slamming back into the wall. Samuel's fingers were like steel and Ryan's vision clouded, dimmed, and a distant part of him knew he was about to pass out.

The window exploded. Ryan dropped. He sucked in air and his head pounded. There was movement all around him. Foe flew backwards over the couch. Skulduggery was there, flipping Mercy over his hip. The door came down, on top of Obloquy. Valkyrie, clambering over it, shouting at Ryan to run. Ryan's legs, like concrete. Around him shouts and curses and the sound of breaking things. Samuel, hitting Valkyrie so hard she folded in mid-air. Foe diving at Skulduggery.

The floor moved and Ryan realised he was stumbling. He didn't even remember ordering his legs to do it. He climbed over the door, slid down it, rolled out into the corridor. Got to his hands and knees, trying to get his brain back in gear.

"Oh God oh God," he muttered, and stood, walked and ran, ran down to the corner, through the corridor, running for the stairs, leaving Skulduggery and Valkyrie to fight behind him. He got to the stairs and stopped. He couldn't. He couldn't leave them. They'd saved his life. He had this stupid key imprinted on to his hand and they were fighting to protect him. He couldn't abandon them. He had to help. There was nothing he could do, but he had to help. He had to try. He had to do something. They would want him to run, he knew that. They would want him to run to safety, to leave the fighting to the professionals. They didn't expect him to turn back and help. But he had no choice.

Ryan turned, ran back the way he had come. An old man was in the corridor, blinking.

"I've phoned the police," he said.

"Get back inside," Ryan told him. "Lock the door."

The old man nodded, shuffled out of the corridor, and then Valkyrie came crashing through the wall of his apartment in a shower of broken plaster and chipboard. The old man howled in shock, ran past Ryan, sprinting round the corner with surprising agility. Valkyrie was on the floor in a cloud of dust, groaning and trying to get up. Obloquy climbed through the broken wall after her and saw Ryan.

"Run!" Valkyrie shouted.

Ryan ran.

He got to the corner before he heard Obloquy's voice in his head – *pain, feel pain, too much pain to move* – and Ryan staggered, doubled up, sweat breaking out on his forehead. He looked back, saw Obloquy, and now he dropped to his knees, trying not to cry out. The pain was building, intensifying, the closer Obloquy got to him, and then Valkyrie was there, covered in dust and swinging both arms, and the pain went away as Obloquy hurtled into the wall.

Mercy stepped out behind her and Ryan shouted a warning, but even as Valkyrie spun, Mercy was opening her mouth, and that red stream of energy slammed straight into Valkyrie's chest, throwing her back. Skulduggery leaped from nowhere, barging into Mercy, and Ryan scrambled over to Valkyrie, his eyes wide, expecting to see a gaping, bloody hole. But when she came to a groaning stop, there was no injury – just trails of steam that rose from her jacket. He grabbed her, pulled her up.

There were gunshots, and with every deafening bang, Ryan yelped and flinched, but he managed to drag Valkyrie round the corner before either of them was horribly killed. She straightened up, taking a deep breath and rubbing her chest.

He had to ask. "Why aren't you dead?"

"Protective clothing," she said, eyes scanning the corridor. "You don't think I wear this outfit just because it's tight, do you?"

She ran to the window at the end of the corridor, flattened both hands against the air. The glass exploded outwards and the frame splintered. "Come on," she said, climbing on to the narrow sill.

"Uh," Ryan said.

She looked back in. "Move!"

He swallowed, and did what she ordered. As he searched for the securest position possible, fingers curling round the edge of the wall, he tried not to look at the concrete courtyard below them. "We're... we're not going to jump, are we?"

She took hold of his arm, and said gently, "Not if you don't want to."

He relaxed, his grip on the edge of the wall loosening slightly, and that's when she stepped off the sill and yanked him after her.

Ryan screamed as they plummeted to the ground, the wind rushing into his mouth and up his nose and through his hair and suddenly it was buffeting them both, slowing their descent. He saw Valkyrie's hand move, like she was orchestrating the air. They landed heavily, but at least they didn't go splat.

Ryan staggered away from her. "Oh my God. Oh my God."

Skulduggery dropped down in front of him and Ryan screamed again.

"Well said," Skulduggery muttered, reloading his revolver. "We'd better hurry, now. Come along."

They ran through the tunnel connecting the courtyard to the street on the other side of the apartment buildings. Skulduggery put his gun away and let his façade flow over his skull. They got in the Bentley and the car roared and shot forward.

"Everyone OK?" Skulduggery asked.

"I'm in pain," Valkyrie groaned. "Ryan?"

Ryan nodded quickly. "I'm fine. I'm OK. I'm not hurt."

"Are you shaking yet?"

Ryan looked at his hand. "No."

"It'll start any minute now."

Ryan's hand began to tremble violently. "Oh wow, yeah. I'm definitely shaking now." He laughed. It was a weird sound.

"Geoffrey's going to have his hands full explaining this one," Valkyrie said as she brushed the dust off her jacket. It rose from her in small clouds.

"Please don't do that in the car," Skulduggery said.

"You didn't tell me Mercy could do that," Ryan said. "She changed shape. She's a shape-changer."

"Actually," Skulduggery said, "she's not. Francine was a psychic image. Basically, an illusion. Physically, there *was* no disguise. That was Mercy sitting at the table, talking to us, in her normal form. But our minds reinterpreted Mercy as Francine. We heard Francine's voice."

"I smelled her perfume," Ryan said.

"All an illusion. The only person in Dublin, in all of Ireland really, capable of disguising her like that is a man called Robert Crasis. In wartime, his skills were invaluable. We might have twenty people ready to storm an enemy position, but thanks to Crasis it would look like we had a thousand."

"So he's a good guy?" Valkyrie asked. "Then why did he help Foe?"

"I don't know," Skulduggery said. "I suppose we'll have to ask him."

SIX

On the way to see Crasis, they stopped off so Ryan and Valkyrie could get something to eat. They each bought a Coke and a sandwich, but Skulduggery made them eat with their heads sticking out of the window to avoid crumbs being dropped. Ryan didn't dare open his Coke in case it fizzed out over the seats, and by the time the Bentley pulled over, his throat was parched.

Skulduggery led the way to an old workshop in a quiet part of town. He knocked on the door and waited. When Robert Crasis opened the door, he looked at Skulduggery and Valkyrie, but barely glanced at Ryan. He was a man in his sixties. He was tall, broad-shouldered. His hair was grey, his jaw coated in stubble.

"Can I help you?"

"Hello Robert," said Skulduggery. "Mind if we come in?"

"Skulduggery?" Crasis frowned, peering at him. "Since when do you have a face?"

"It's a relatively new addition. We'd like a word, if that's OK."

Crasis hesitated, then stepped back to allow them through the door.

They walked into a carpenter's workshop, to the smell of wood shavings and varnish. It was a big space, no windows, lit in spots that allowed the darkness to soak in around the edges.

Skulduggery let his face melt away, and he took off his hat and looked around. "This reminds me of your place in Venice."

"Before it was burned down," Crasis responded.

"Skulduggery, I don't mean to be rude, but I was really hoping never to see you again."

"You know why we're here."

Crasis shook his head. The muscles in his jaw tightened. "All I want is to be left alone. I'm out of that game, but people... people keep pulling me back in. After years of not being involved in any craziness, suddenly there's one after another, when all I want to do is be a carpenter and grow old."

"You *want* to get old?" Valkyrie asked, sounding surprised.

"Staying young isn't all it's cracked up to be," Crasis said. "I've been young and strong and healthy for two hundred years. I've had to leave my home countless times to stop my mortal friends from wondering why I never seem to age. Then I met Sarah, and she became my wife, and suddenly I had someone I wanted to grow old with. So I stopped doing magic. Up until two weeks ago, I hadn't done magic in nearly fifteen years. I went grey. Last month I noticed a bald spot. It was working. I was ageing again. But now? Now it'll take me years to age a *day*."

"This last job you did," Skulduggery said, "it was for Mercy Charient, wasn't it?"

Crasis nodded. "They came in the back, the whole lot of them. Deacon Maybury, the idiot, had mentioned what I used to do for the Sanctuary, and they remembered. Of course they remembered. So they came in, threatened me, threatened my wife, my kids... What could I do?"

"We're not blaming you," Skulduggery said.

"So I did it. I made her into a frumpy little woman. It wasn't my best work, but it would do for a few hours, which is all they wanted it for. Sorry if any of you were hurt, but I have a family to protect."

"We weren't hurt," Valkyrie said. "But Deacon Maybury... he was killed a few days ago."

Crasis looked at her for a moment, saying nothing. He swallowed, and nodded. "That's a shame," he said, his eyes drifting down. "He was... I'd like to say he was a good man, but he was... Deacon. I owed him, though. He's the one who actually introduced me to Sarah. He'd asked her out the previous week and she'd laughed so hard she fell over. It was love at first sight for Sarah and me. So I owed him, I did. It's a …it's a real pity I'll never get to repay him."

Ryan tried opening his Coke quietly. It fizzed and they all looked at him. He blushed.

"Maybe you can repay him," Skulduggery said, looking back at Crasis. "When you were working on Mercy, did any of them say anything? They have the Doomsday Machine hidden away somewhere and we need to find it."

"Foe has the Doomsday Machine?" Crasis said, his eyes widening. "And Deacon was working with those guys?"

"He planned to sell the key to whoever paid him enough," Valkyrie said.

Crasis stared at her, stared at Skulduggery, stared at Ryan, then stared at his hands. "It's a good thing he's dead," he said. "Because if I had the chance, I'd kill him myself. I did hear something, actually. I heard Obloquy complain that there were always people around whenever they'd check on 'it'. They never said what it was, but obviously it was the Machine. Mercy was supposed to stay still and quiet while I worked, but she kept moving and joining in with the conversation. She was joking that if their car broke down, they'd all have to get the Luas. She said they'd be riding the tram to the end of the world. I told her to shut up or I'd have to start again. I should have let her keep talking."

"You wouldn't happen to have a street map of Dublin, would you?" Skulduggery asked.

"Uh, yeah," Crasis said. "I think I have one somewhere around here."

He went off to search, and Skulduggery picked up a thick felt pen off a desk that was littered with paperwork. "They've hidden the Machine in a public place," he said, "and it's somewhere on or near a tram line."

Crasis came back with a tattered map and laid it out on a large, freshly carved table. Skulduggery started drawing lines down streets, drawing in the routes the Luas tram went down. Crasis and Valkyrie pored over the map and Ryan, not wanting to feel left out, did the same. He put his Coke on the table and did his best to appear as smart as the other people in the room.

When Skulduggery had marked all the routes they examined the map anew.

"Lot of public places," Valkyrie murmured.

"A very large amount," Ryan said, nodding like he was contributing.

"Ryan," Skulduggery said, and for a moment Ryan thought that he'd accidentally solved the mystery.

"Yes?" he said eagerly.

"Could you take your Coke off the map, please?"

"Oh," Ryan said. "Sorry." He lifted his bottle. There was now a wet circle around Dundrum. To hide his blush he took a long swig from his drink.

"The heaviest population centres would be here, here and here," Skulduggery said, marking the map with Xs. "If the Machine is hidden outdoors, we should be looking for areas that have had extensive construction work in the last few years. If it's indoors, then we're looking for new public buildings or shopping areas."

The Coke went down the wrong way and Ryan choked, gagged, and spat a mouthful all over the map.

Skulduggery, Crasis and Valkyrie looked at him.

"Sorry," he wheezed, before doubling over into a coughing fit.

"Maybe you should get some air," Skulduggery suggested.

Ryan nodded, coughing too much to respond, and staggered out of the door. His eyes were streaming and he knew his face was glowing an attractive shade of red. He went to the Bentley and leaned against it, finally getting the coughing under control. Not his finest moment.

"How're you doing, Ryan?"

He looked around as Valkyrie walked up.

"I'm OK," he said. "Just choking a bit. Sorry about that. I hope I didn't spit any on you."

"Don't worry about it."

He became aware of her looking at him and he looked away.

"Why do you do that?" she asked.

"Why do I do what?"

"Why do you look away whenever I look at you?"

"Um," Ryan said, "I don't know. I think, once I realise that I'm looking someone in the eye, I forget how long I'm supposed to do it. So, I don't know, I suppose I look away before it gets weird."

She smiled. "You're an oddball."

"Yeah," he said, sagging.

Valkyrie didn't notice the sag. She was looking up the street, watching the people pass. "But that's OK. We're all oddballs here."

Now that she wasn't paying attention, he could look at her. He liked her face. She was very pretty, had a cute nose and a single dimple when she smiled. He'd always wanted a girlfriend like her – someone impressive, someone confident. He'd like to go back to school once the summer was over and have her beside him. Then everyone would stop and stare, and they'd think to themselves that there must be more to this Ryan guy after all.

But he'd never get a girlfriend like her. He

knew that. Girls like Valkyrie saw him as a friend only. They went off with the good-looking guys or the cool guys or the guys who didn't make fools of themselves at regular intervals. A girl like Valkyrie would never be impressed with someone like Ryan.

He looked away before she looked back. He didn't want her to catch him watching.

"You're coping pretty well, you know," she said, facing him again. "When I first saw Skulduggery and all this stuff, I freaked. I actually blacked out."

"You fainted?"

"No," she said, her good humour fading. "I blacked out. There's a difference."

He grinned. "You fainted."

"Shut up. You're handling this well, that's all I'm saying. You haven't once asked to go home."

His grin went away. "Why would I? You're not that much older than me, you know."

She frowned. "What's that got to do with anything?"

"I'm fifteen. You're, I don't know, seventeen?"

"So?"

"That's only two years' difference," Ryan said hotly. "We're practically the same age and you're treating me like I'm a child. Fine, OK? You have no interest in me. I'm used to that. But don't stand there and talk down to me like you're so much better than I am."

Valkyrie looked at him and didn't say anything. He started to feel stupid.

Then she folded her arms and tilted her hips and it only got worse. "First of all," she said, "I'm not talking down to you *or* treating you like a child."

"But you expect me to want to go home."

"Of course I do. You were attacked. You're in danger. You're hanging around with people who can do magic. You've had what we call in the business a shock. Usually, when people get a shock they want to retreat to a safe place so that they can process what they've seen. Most people would want to go home right now. But not you. You haven't mentioned home, haven't mentioned your family, haven't tried to run off or call the cops. You are coping well, Ryan. That's all I said. That's all I meant. I have no idea what our ages have to do with anything or what you're talking about when you say I have no interest."

"Oh," he said.

"And the only time you have actually acted like a child," she said, "is right now. I don't like petulance, Ryan. I don't respond well to it."

"Right."

"When it comes to this kind of stuff, I'm the only one who is allowed to sulk. Skulduggery understands that. Do you?"

"Yes," he said, nodding quickly. "I'm sorry."

"You better be."

"I really am."

"I gave you a compliment and you jumped down my throat." She narrowed her eyes at him. "And what was all that about having no interest? Having no interest in what?"

"Uh, nothing."

"Don't make me hit you, Ryan."

He winced. "I don't know, I was just... I thought you saw me as a, you know, as a kid and... I was just saying, that while, obviously, you'd never, like, go out with someone like me, that's still no reason to talk down to me. Which you weren't doing, and I apologise again for thinking you were."

"But what does me going out or not going out with someone like you have to do with anything?"

Ryan tried a smile. "I really don't know any more. It made sense when I said it."

She shook her head, looked about to say something else, then stopped. "Oh," she said. She was looking at him now like Andrea from school had looked at him when he'd asked her to the movies. She was looking at him with a kind of gentle pity.

"It's OK," he said. "You don't have to worry about it."

"Ryan, we only just met."

He nodded. "Absolutely."

"It's not that I never would," Valkyrie said, "but I generally go for guys... older than me, you know?"

Ryan tried a laugh. "Like vampires."

Her tone turned sharp. "We don't joke about vampires, Ryan."

"Right. Sorry."

"I think you're nice," Valkyrie said, softening again. "But let's concentrate on being friends for the time being, all right?"

"Sure. Yep. Don't worry."

The workshop door opened and Skulduggery emerged. "Ryan," he said, "stop leaning against my car."

"Sorry," Ryan mumbled, straightening up.

Skulduggery stopped in front of them. He was wearing a different face, and he put his hat on. "I have solved the mystery," he announced. "Before I take you to where the Doomsday Machine is located, I would like you both to acknowledge how brilliant I am."

"Uh," said Ryan, "you're brilliant."

"You're OK," said Valkyrie.

"That's good enough for me," Skulduggery nodded. "Get in the car. We've got a world to save."

SEVEN

They drove into Dundrum Town Centre and parked in the multi-storey. Along the way, Skulduggery had pulled over three times to allow Ryan to pee. If Ryan had wanted Valkyrie to start thinking of him as older and more mature than he was, he knew he was not going about it the right way.

Once the Bentley found a place to park, they got out.

"How did you know it was here?" Valkyrie asked.

Skulduggery checked his façade in the wing

mirror, then straightened up. "Simple detective work," he said. "We're going to need somewhere quiet to wait until everyone's gone. We'll search for the Machine tonight, dismantle it and then it'll all be over."

They started walking. "Shouldn't we call in the Cleavers?" Valkyrie asked. "We'll find it faster with a hundred people looking for it."

"I'd prefer to approach this with a little more delicacy," Skulduggery said. "The three of us should be fine." He looked at Ryan. "Nervous?"

"A little," Ryan admitted. "What if Foe and the others are waiting for us?"

"They might pay a visit to the Machine," Skulduggery conceded, "but they're not going to be lying in wait. They have no idea that we know it's here."

They passed from the car park into the mall. Valkyrie appeared to trust Skulduggery without hesitation, but Ryan was more cautious. Every time someone walked too close, he'd hop away, waiting for their image to flicker and drop, revealing

Mercy or Obloquy or Foe. But the people in the mall seemed to be actual people, focused on their conversations or their shopping, and the only time they glanced at Ryan was when he stumbled awkwardly away from them.

Valkyrie raised an eyebrow at him. "You're not very good at acting casual."

"I forget how," Ryan confessed, skipping away from a suspicious-looking two-year-old holding a balloon.

Skulduggery and Valkyrie walked up the travelator and Ryan followed, flinching away from an elderly woman with a wrinkled prune-face. They approached a stocky security guard.

"Excuse me, good sir," Skulduggery began.

The security guard turned to them. "I'm a woman," she said.

"And a fetching one you are too," Skulduggery continued, smiling. "Which way to the security control room?"

The security guard frowned. "Why? What business do you have there? Who are you?"

"All good questions," Skulduggery said, nodding, "and all questions I would love to answer. Unfortunately, we only have time for *one* answer, and since my question was the *first* and, let's be honest, the most *important* question, I feel that it is the question that deserves an answer. So, your security control room?"

The security guard folded her arms. "Do you have the authority to be there?"

Skulduggery's false face fixed her with a glare. "Do I have the authority?" he repeated. "Do *I* have the *authority*? Tell me, my dear, do I not *look* like I have the authority? Do I not *look* like the type of person who goes wherever he sees fit to go? Or do I look like the kind of person who needs *permission* to do the things that need to be done?"

"Uh," said the security guard, her arms no longer folded.

Skulduggery loomed over her. "There are things in this world that would turn your hair *white*. Threats and dangers to your very way of life that would send you shrieking into the corner to tremble and sob. Someone needs to protect the world from these dangers and threats. Is that someone going to be you? Is it? Because if it is, my companions and I will leave, right now, and entrust to you our continued survival. But if you have doubts, if you think you might falter right when you are needed to make the ultimate sacrifice, then tell us now and step back, for saving the world is what we do, and we're really very good at it."

The security guard's lip trembled, and she pointed to a door. "That way," she said. "Turn left."

Skulduggery clamped a hand on to her shoulder. "You are doing fine work," he told her, and led the way to the door. When they were through he walked past the left turn, to a room at the end of the concrete corridor. Inside was a table and two chairs. Ryan reckoned this must be where they kept shoplifters while they waited for the cops to arrive.

"We shouldn't be bothered in here," Skulduggery said, closing the door behind them. His false face melted away as he looked at his pocket watch.

"Three hours until closing. Make yourselves comfortable."

He sat at the table and took off his hat. Ryan and Valkyrie remained standing.

"I still don't understand why they want to destroy the world," said Ryan. "Foe said he couldn't see the point of life but, I mean, that's a really *silly* reason..."

"They're bad guys," Valkyrie told him. "Villains. Some villains have proper plans. Others don't. They've just been around for a few hundred years. Given enough time, a stray thought can become an obsession, and then a purpose. They're nuts, Ryan. They're actually insane people who all agree with one another."

"Insanity fuels insanity," Skulduggery said, nodding, "just as stupidity fuels stupidity."

"Speaking of stupidity," Valkyrie said, "I'm just going to ask this one more time and you better give me an answer, because I haven't a clue how you worked it out. How do we know the Machine is here?"

A moment passed before Skulduggery spoke again. "Ryan told me," he said.

Ryan looked at him. "I told you what?"

Skulduggery raised his head, and he looked at Ryan with those hollow eye sockets. "You told me the Machine was hidden in Dundrum. Completely unconsciously, of course. You tried to hide Dundrum on the map with your bottle of Coke, then you tried to distract us with a coughing fit."

"Uh," Ryan said, "what?"

"The drive over confirmed it. Stopping three times to relieve yourself? You were only delaying the inevitable."

"No I wasn't," Ryan said. "What are you talking about? How would I know where the Machine was hidden?"

"And why would Ryan be trying to stop us from finding it?" Valkyrie asked.

Skulduggery hesitated. "Ryan, why haven't you asked to go home?"

Ryan frowned, genuinely and completely puzzled. "What?"

"You haven't asked to go home," Skulduggery said. "You haven't tried to *call* home to tell them you're OK, even though they must be worried about you by now."

Ryan glowered, angry at having to admit this in front of Valkyrie. "I'm... I'm running away."

Valkyrie's eyes widened. "What? Why?"

"It's a long story."

"No it isn't," said Skulduggery.

Valkyrie swatted the skeleton's arm. "Skulduggery, shut up. Ryan, what's wrong?"

"My... my dad died. My mum remarried. He's an OK guy but... I don't like being in that house. It reminds me—"

"No it doesn't," Skulduggery said.

"Stop interrupting!" Ryan shouted. "You don't know what it's like! You don't know!"

"You don't know either," Skulduggery said. "I'm really sorry to have to tell you this, Ryan, but the reason you don't want to go home is because there is no home to go to. Ryan, you're not real. You don't exist."

Ryan stared at him. "What?"

"You're Deacon Maybury," Skulduggery said. "You're a hiding place who thinks it's a boy."

EIGHT

Ryan backed away. "You're crazy."

"I am," Skulduggery said. "I'm also right. Deacon planned this whole thing – as much as he could, anyway. He hid the key, faked his own death and then went to Crasis – called in that old favour. He told Crasis to make him look inconspicuous – someone Foe would never suspect of having anything to do with any of this."

"Skulduggery," Valkyrie said softly. "Are you sure?"

"Crasis only looked at Ryan twice in the whole

time we were there. He wanted to tell us, but I expect he'd made a promise to stay quiet. Once his new image was in place, Deacon went to work on his own mind. He couldn't take the chance that Obloquy would be able to read his thoughts. He had to disappear completely. He subdued his personality and replaced it with Ryan – a good boy. A decent person."

"You're wrong," Ryan said. "I don't know what you're talking about, but you're wrong."

"I wish I was," Skulduggery said, "but I rarely am. Deacon planned to hide away until Foe lost his trail. Ryan, can you remember what you did this morning?"

"I got up," Ryan said. "Had breakfast with my mum."

"Again, I'm sorry to tell you, but that's a false memory. The person you think is your mother doesn't exist."

Ryan had an ache, somewhere in his chest. "No. She's my mum. She's my mum and I love her."

"I know you do," Skulduggery said. "Deacon is

very thorough. But there's only so much a Sensitive can do to suppress a personality, especially when he works on himself. Cracks start to show much earlier. That's why you were at the library today. Somewhere in your subconscious, you knew it was important. You knew exactly where to find that key."

Ryan realised he was crying. He wiped away tears.

"When we were looking at the map, you knew we wanted to dismantle the Machine. Your subconscious didn't want that. So it tried to block our way here."

"You're wrong," Ryan said.

"I'm right. You know I'm right."

"No. No you're not. I know who I am."

"Which is why you're crying."

"No," Ryan said. "Shut up. Stop it. I know who I am. I'm me. What you're saying is stupid. It's ridiculous. I'd know if I wasn't me. I'd know it."

"No you wouldn't. And I'm very sorry."

*

They hadn't spoken to him in three hours. They sat over there, at the table. Occasionally, he'd hear them talking softly. They were giving him space.

From somewhere outside, he could hear the announcements, alerting shoppers that the mall was closing. He imagined all the friends and families hurrying out, chatting and laughing and mothers dragging kids and kids wailing and crying...

Ryan remembered being a kid. He remembered his mum. And his dad. He remembered how much he loved his mum, and how much he missed his dad. He didn't want to run away any more. He wanted to go home. But the more he thought about going home, the less real it became.

It was dark in the room when Valkyrie came over. She sat on the ground beside him, her back against the wall.

"Hey Ryan," she said, her voice quiet.

"That's not my name," he told her. His own voice shook like it always did when he was emotional. At least, that's what he remembered.

"I'm going to call you Ryan until I can't call you Ryan any more," Valkyrie said. "I don't care about Deacon. I've never met him. I don't know him. I know you, Ryan. And I like you."

He nodded. Didn't answer.

"We're going to go looking for the Machine now," she said. "We have a few hours before the cleaning crews get here. Skulduggery thinks dismantling the bomb won't be a problem. Do you still want to do it?"

Ryan tried to see her pretty face in the gloom. "What would you do if I didn't? Would you cut off my hand and dismantle it yourself? How do you know you can trust me? I'm Deacon, after all."

"You're still you."

"There *is* no me."

Her hand found his. Despite himself, Ryan's heartbeat quickened. "We all have a side to ourselves that we don't like," she said. "Skulduggery has one. I have one. Now you have one. But you don't have to be ruled by it. You can make your own choices, Ryan. Deacon wants to sell the Machine – to make some money and then leave the mess for someone else to deal with. You want to take it apart so that nobody can ever use it. You can choose to help us. You can choose to help *me*."

"And me," Skulduggery said from the other side of the room.

"Shut up," Valkyrie said, not turning away from Ryan.

"Right," said Skulduggery.

The ghost of a smile found its way on to Ryan's lips. "If I do help you," he said, "that would really annoy Deacon, wouldn't it?"

"Oh," said Valkyrie, "it would."

Ryan liked that idea. It was the only way he could think of to have his revenge on a man who had snatched away a family and a life that were never real in the first place. But Ryan's hurt was real. His pain was real. And for the next few hours, at least, Ryan himself was determined that he himself would be real.

"I have one condition," Ryan said.

He saw the outline of Valkyrie's head tilting to

one side. "OK," she said cautiously.

"If I do this, and I dismantle the bomb, can I kiss you?"

He felt her slow, slow smile. "We'll have to see about that," she said, and got up. She pulled him to his feet.

Skulduggery led the way out into the mall. The shops themselves were dark and shuttered, but the main strip of the mall was still lit. It was odd, being in a space designed for crowds and seeing it empty. It didn't fit. It wasn't right. It was, all of a sudden, incredibly lonely.

They walked down the deactivated travelator, no one talking. They reached the ground floor and Ryan wandered around, his hand held open in front of him. Skulduggery had insisted that once he got close to the Machine, he'd start to feel something. A buzzing, maybe. A tingle. Ryan had asked if it would be sore. Skulduggery couldn't promise anything.

Valkyrie walked behind him. She pitied him. He

knew she did. Of course she did. Who wouldn't? He was a pitiful person who wasn't even a person. He didn't even know what he looked like, not really. He knew he wasn't fifteen. He knew he was older. He wondered what colour hair he had. He wondered what his face was like. How his voice sounded. He wondered what his thoughts were like. The only thing he knew was that he wasn't a very nice person – not really. Not truly. A nice person wouldn't do something like this.

His hand tingled. Slight pins and needles. "I think we're close," he said. His words sounded weird in this place.

"It's below us," said Skulduggery, "built into the foundations. There's an activation panel somewhere around here. Follow the buzzing."

Ryan did as he was told, and led them to a section of the wall. Skulduggery tapped it with his knuckle. It sounded normal to Ryan, but Skulduggery obviously heard something that he didn't. It must have been great to be Skulduggery – to always know what to do, to always know what needed to be done.

Even in the false life Deacon Maybury had given him, Ryan had never known that kind of certainty.

"Why didn't he make me better?" he asked as Skulduggery continued to tap.

Valkyrie looked at him. "What do you mean?"

Ryan's laugh came out of nowhere and didn't last long. "I mean, look at me. Why didn't he make me cooler, or smarter, or better-looking? He was creating a whole new person, right? So why did he make him as rubbish as me?"

"You're... you're not rubbish, Ryan."

"Yes I am. I'm fat and ugly and useless."

"Skulduggery," Valkyrie said, "tell him."

Skulduggery stopped tapping the wall, and looked at Ryan. "Deacon made someone who would blend in with the background, someone too unexceptional to notice."

Valkyrie shook her head. "You're meant to make him feel better."

"I'm about to," Skulduggery said. "He made you unexceptional, Ryan. He made you normal. As normal as he could. And in doing so, he has single-handedly proven how exceptional normal people can be. When we were at Deacon's apartment, you could have run and left Valkyrie and myself to fight them off ourselves. But you turned back. You turned back to help. You stood up to terrifying people who want to kill the world, who would snap you in two and tear you apart and not lose one wink of sleep over it, and you did so without training or magic. You did so because you are a good person, and you have true courage. You have the kind of courage Deacon Maybury himself never had. He made you the most normal boy he could, and he inadvertently made you so much better than he could ever hope to be."

"Oh," Valkyrie said, "well... OK, that's better than I thought it was going to be. How are you feeling now, Ryan?"

Ryan looked at her. "I'm feeling pretty special, actually," he said, and she laughed.

Skulduggery pressed his thumbs into the wall, and a large section slid to one side. Instead of the mass of wires that Ryan expected, however, there was a carving of the key in the centre of what looked like a complicated metal maze.

"Oh good," Skulduggery said.

Valkyrie peered closer. "Is it going to be easy to dismantle?"

"Not in the slightest."

"Do you think you can manage it?"

Skulduggery tapped his chin. "Only with an inordinate amount of luck."

"So we should probably wait for an expert."

"Good God, no," Skulduggery said, jerking his head around. "Where's the fun in that?"

"But... but if you get it wrong, we might all die."

"Yes, that is true, but I probably won't get it wrong."

Valkyrie's eyes flickered to Ryan, then back to Skulduggery. "You probably won't?"

"The odds are in my favour."

"Really?"

"Almost."

"I vote we wait for an expert."

"But that might take twenty minutes or *longer*, Valkyrie."

"So? It's not like it's counting down or anything. We have all the time in the world."

"And there's no time like the present. Ryan, I'm going to need you to press your hand against the carving. I'll guide you every step of the way from then on."

Valkyrie's tone was firm. "Skulduggery. We are calling this in and then we're waiting for a bomb-disposal expert."

"What will he know that I don't?"

"About the disposal of bombs? Lots."

Skulduggery waved a hand dismissively. "Bombs are simple things. They're designed to go off. What we have to do in order to thwart the bomb is to *stop* it from going off. What could be more straightforward?"

Valkyrie's fingers closed round Ryan's wrist and she pulled him away. "We are waiting for an expert."

"I think we should let him try," said a voice from

behind them. They spun, saw Foe and his gang walking up. Foe was grinning. "It might save us the bother of destroying the world ourselves."

NINE

Valkyrie stepped in front of Ryan, and Skulduggery straightened his tie. "Excellent," he said. "You've fallen right into our trap."

Foe looked around at the otherwise empty mall, eyebrow raised. "This is a trap, is it? So this is the bit where all the Cleavers appear? This is the part where we surrender due to being completely outnumbered and you cart us off to our cells?"

"Roughly, yes."

Foe's grin grew wider. "Has the trap been sprung yet?"

"I'm simply not going to dignify that with an answer," said Skulduggery.

Standing behind Obloquy, Samuel was sweating badly. Ryan could see the lines of tension on his face. He looked to be in pain.

"Your pet doesn't look too good," Valkyrie said.

Foe glanced back, then shrugged. "When the sun goes down, all a vampire wants to do is rip off his skin and kill everything in sight. Right now, the only thing keeping all of us safe is the last drop of a serum he took. Your boyfriend took something similar, didn't he? What was his name? Caelan?"

Valkyrie's shoulders stiffened and her voice grew harder. "He was *not* my boyfriend."

"Bad break-up, was it? Actually, don't answer that. I heard it was. Bad for him more than you, though, wasn't it?"

"We don't talk about vampires," Ryan muttered.

Foe smiled and Mercy laughed. "See?" she said. "Told you he fancies her."

"So what if he does?" Valkyrie snapped back. "He's a nice guy. After we've smacked you lot around, we may as well give it a go. What's the matter, Mercy – jealous that two people can like each other when nobody in their right mind would ever like you?"

Mercy glared. "Plenty have liked me."

"Yeah," Valkyrie said, "I've heard."

The glare turned to a scowl. "Not like that."

"You don't have to justify yourself to me."

"Says the girl who dated a vampire."

"Says the psycho who dated everyone."

"Detective Pleasant," Foe said, interrupting the conversation just when it was getting interesting, "you've gone suspiciously quiet. It's not like you to miss an argument."

"Carry on," Skulduggery said, his head down, "don't mind me..."

Foe frowned. "What are you doing?"

Skulduggery waited a moment, then looked up, and showed them his phone. "Just sending a message. Reinforcements should be here soon."

Obloquy sagged. "I told you we should have just attacked them," he rumbled. "But no, you wanted to talk and trade witty banter."

"Shut up, Obloquy," Foe said. "Fine, Detective. You want to skip straight to business? Fine with me. Kill them."

Valkyrie pushed Ryan back slightly as Obloquy headed for her and Mercy zeroed in on Skulduggery.

"Oh sure," Valkyrie said, "I'll take the big one, no problem."

Foe stayed where he was, his eyes on Ryan. Behind him, Samuel sweated.

Mercy opened her mouth and Skulduggery ducked the stream of energy that carved a furrow across the wall behind him. He dodged behind a pillar, but the stream intensified, melting right through the pillar and taking Skulduggery's hat off his head.

Obloquy pressed his hands to his temples and he squeezed, like he wanted to pop his own head open. Valkyrie staggered. She fell to one knee, bringing up her own hands like she was trying to shield herself. Ryan wanted to run and help, but now Foe was walking towards him.

"This doesn't have to hurt," Foe said.

Ryan turned, ran up the still travelator, swung around at the top and ran up the next one. He was halfway up when he started to seriously regret his choice. His legs were already screaming at him and his lungs were burning. He'd never been able to run for any length of time – not even in the school that he remembered but had never actually attended.

He glanced down, saw Skulduggery waving a hand and Mercy flying backwards. Valkyrie was on both knees now, with Obloquy standing directly over her. Darkness pulsed from the ring on her finger and Obloquy jerked back in shock. His psychic attack must have faltered, because Valkyrie immediately wrapped an arm around each leg. She pressed her shoulder against his belly and as she lifted she launched herself forward. Obloquy yelled as he hit the ground, Valkyrie on top, and Ryan saw her first headbutt go in before he reached the top floor and lost her to sight.

Staggering slightly, Ryan ran on, no idea where he was going or what he would do when he got there. The mall was terrifying at night. The few lights that were on cast the deepest shadows. Anyone could be hiding in those shadows.

Foe stepped out ahead of him and Ryan yelled and changed course and ran into a potted plant, tripped over it and sprawled on to the floor.

"I'd ask you to activate the Machine," Foe said, walking up, "but I don't have the time for an argument. So I'm going to be rude. I hope you don't mind, me being rude. It's nothing personal. I'm not going to kill you. Don't think I'm going to kill you. I'm just going to cut off your hand a little bit. You might die from blood loss or trauma or shock – let's not kid ourselves – but you will not die from me cutting off your hand. When you think about it like that, you have nothing to fear from me or my giant knife."

Foe took a machete from his jacket.

Ryan crawled away on his hands and knees,

panting too hard to get up.

"I know some people say they like the thrill of the chase," Foe said, stepping on Ryan's ankle and pinning it there, "but I'm not one of those people. The only thing I care about is ending this world."

Ryan collapsed, and rolled over on to his back. "Why?" he gasped. "Why do you want to... want to kill everyone?"

Foe looked down at him, and shrugged. "Because it's Wednesday."

The machete swung down and Ryan screamed and Skulduggery crashed into Foe from behind. They both went stumbling off. Ryan sat up, looking at his hand, making sure it was still there. He realised he was still screaming so he stopped that and looked around. Skulduggery kicked at Foe's knee, grabbed his head when he bent forward and cracked it against a narrow pillar. Foe staggered and swung a fist, but Skulduggery stepped inside the swing, latched on and started hitting him with elbows. It was all very violent. Ryan's mother, if she'd existed, would not have approved.

"Skulduggery!" Valkyrie shouted from below them.

"Ryan," Skulduggery muttered, as Foe grabbed him round the waist and slammed him back against the wall, "could you take a look and see what she's shouting about now?"

Ryan got up, hurried to the railing, looked over. Mercy and Obloquy were down and not moving, but Valkyrie was backing away from Samuel, who was lurching towards her, bent over like he had stomach cramps.

Ryan looked back. Foe had his arm wrapped around Skulduggery's neck from behind, and he was dragging him like he wanted to pull Skulduggery's head from his spinal column. Skulduggery twisted but Foe adapted, turning his hold into a headlock. Skulduggery reached up, his gloved fingers digging into Foe's eyes. Foe jerked away and lost his grip and Skulduggery pushed against him, tripping him with a sneaky sweep to the ankle. Foe went down and Skulduggery landed on top of him.

"Well?" Skulduggery asked as he pounded Foe with punches.

"Uh, I don't know," said Ryan. "Samuel looks like he's about to throw up."

Surprisingly, Skulduggery and Foe stopped fighting and they both looked over.

"He's doubled over?" Foe asked, panting for breath.

"Yeah," said Ryan.

Foe looked at Skulduggery, and they both stood up.

"You're on your own," Foe said, and ran.

Ryan frowned, looked down at Samuel again. Samuel's moan of pain drifted up, and then suddenly it turned to a growl. Samuel straightened, digging his fingers into his shirt and ripping it open. No, not just his shirt. His skin, too. Samuel ripped his flesh and his clothes from his body, from the bone-white body that lay beneath. His hands, and even from where he stood, Ryan could see the claws on those hands, tore Samuel's face off and threw it to one side, revealing the smooth head and big black eyes and jagged, jagged teeth.

Valkyrie turned and ran, and the vampire bounded after her. Something blurred out of the corner of Ryan's eye and suddenly Skulduggery was vaulting over the railing and dropping to the ground far below.

Ryan ran for the travelator, heading down, heading down to help Valkyrie. He heard her cry out and nearly tripped, nearly went head first. There was a crash of breaking glass and Ryan glimpsed Skulduggery disappearing through a shop window. He was almost at the ground floor when he saw her, saw Valkyrie, hurling fireballs and whipping shadows at the vampire that came at her like a wild animal. It twisted in mid-air, avoiding the slash of darkness Valkyrie sent its way. It landed on her, took her down, its claws raking across her body. She gasped and it raked again, and again, trying to get through her protective clothing, trying to rend flesh and puncture skin, trying to draw blood.

"Hey!" Ryan screamed, running into full view

of the monster. "Hey you! Hey! Come and get me! Come on!"

The vampire snapped its head up, snarling.

"I've got what you want!" Ryan shouted, holding up his imprinted palm. If Samuel the man was still in there somewhere, maybe he'd remember why all this was going on in the first place. Maybe he'd remember that Ryan was the real target. Or maybe the vampire would just see an easy kill and—

The vampire leaped off Valkyrie. Ryan howled in terror and started running again. He glanced back in time to see it claws and its teeth and feel the rush of air as it swooped up and over him.

Ryan's feet got mixed up and he tripped over himself. He sat on the ground, looking up. The vampire hung in the air, looking down. It writhed and snarled, slashed at him with its claws.

Skulduggery walked over, hands open, fingers flexing slightly as he held the creature in place. His suit was torn and his tie was crooked. Valkyrie limped over, holding his hat. She showed it to him, and he groaned. There was a large hole burned through the top.

The vampire snarled at them all.

Skulduggery raised his arms, and the vampire rose in the air. Higher and higher it went, up past every floor. Valkyrie took Ryan's arm, escorted him to the benches. When the vampire couldn't rise any higher, Skulduggery dropped his hands quickly, and the vampire plunged downwards.

"This won't kill it," Valkyrie told Ryan as the vampire fell. "But it'll break enough bones to stop it from bothering us."

The vampire hit the ground with a satisfying *thwack*, and didn't get up.

Skulduggery examined his poor hat, and laid it to one side. "Ryan," he said. "I know you've been through a lot, but there is the small matter of dismantling a bomb to get through, and then I'll let you rest. I promise."

TEN

With Skulduggery's guidance, Ryan dismantled the Doomsday Machine. He rendered each and every part of it inert. When it was done, when the last piece was made useless, his hand started to burn. He hissed, looked at his palm, and the imprint faded to nothing.

"Well done, Ryan," Skulduggery said. "You saved the world."

"You knew exactly what to do," Ryan said. "You *did* know how to dismantle it after all."

"I'm glad you got that impression," Skulduggery

said kindly. "But really I could have just as easily killed us all. Still, it's better than waiting around for the experts, isn't it?"

He took a set of handcuffs from his belt and went to shackle the unconscious prisoners, leaving Ryan and Valkyrie alone.

"How long do I have?" Ryan asked.

Valkyrie hesitated. "Skulduggery said... he said that as soon as this was over, one way or the other, Deacon's personality would start to reassert itself."

"So I don't have long," Ryan said quietly.

"I'm... I'm afraid not."

Ryan nodded. He didn't say anything. He didn't trust his voice not to break.

"You probably saved my life back there," Valkyrie said. "That was a very brave thing you did."

Ryan managed a smile. "Maybe it's something you'll remember me for."

"I definitely think so."

"I don't feel very brave right now. To be honest, I kind of feel like crying."

Valkyrie's hand rested on his shoulder.

"I really don't want to die," Ryan said. He was crying now. He didn't care. The only thing he cared about was that in a few moments he wouldn't be here any more. He wouldn't exist. They'd stopped Foe and the others from destroying the world, but Ryan's world was ending just the same. "It's not fair. How come Deacon gets to live and I don't?"

"I don't know," Valkyrie said softly.

"Isn't there anything you can do? Maybe Skulduggery can do something? Maybe he knows someone who can, who can block Deacon from coming back, or..."

"I'm sorry, Ryan," Valkyrie said. She was crying too. This pretty girl with the single dimple when she smiled, she was crying for him. This pretty girl who would never go out with a guy like Ryan, not in a million years, was sitting here with her arm round him, and they were crying together.

He fought to control his sobs. When he could speak, he spoke quietly. "Could I have that kiss now?"

She looked at him. "Definitely," she said, and

leaned in. He turned his head slightly, didn't know if he should close his eyes or keep them open, but when their lips met his eyes closed. His first kiss in fifteen years of false memories. His only kiss in fifteen hours of real life.

They parted. His head was clouded. His thoughts were fuzzy.

"I really like you, Valkyrie," he managed to mumble.

"I really like you, Ryan," she said back to him.

Ryan smiled and tried to kiss her again, this pretty girl with the dimple, what was her name again, Valkyrie, that was it, seventeen years old and cute as a button, the kind of girl who had never even noticed Deacon when he was that age. He grinned and leaned in and felt her hand against his chest, keeping him back, and then her eyes were narrowing.

"Ryan?"

"I'll be whoever you want me to be," Deacon said, and she hit him so hard the whole world spun.

She stood over him. "Get rid of that face," she

said. "Stop using Ryan's face right now or I swear to God I'll batter you."

"OK!" he cried. "Just don't hit me again!"

Deacon got to his feet, his jaw aching. "Ain't that something?" he muttered, and at those words, the image around him flickered and withdrew, and suddenly he was back to his old self again.

Valkyrie's eyes sparkled with tears. She was looking at him like she was going to hit him again anyway.

"I just want to thank you," he said before she did. "I was in a serious bind and you, you came in and you really helped me. I was in over my head, I don't mind admitting it. If it makes any difference, I never intended for the Machine to end up in enemy hands. The moment I sold the key, I was going to alert the Sanctuary and get an army of Cleavers in here to—"

"You risked the lives of everyone on the *planet*," Valkyrie said, her voice tight.

"I did," he said, nodding sadly, "and I truly regret that. It was stupid. It was short-sighted, and selfish. If I knew then what I know now, I would never have tried it. But we all make mistakes, isn't that right? And I made a mistake. A terrible, terrible mistake that could have had untold consequences for—"

He didn't even see the punch. He saw her shoulder shift and then he was toppling backwards. He hit the ground and his face felt three sizes too big. Good *God*, she hit hard.

"You better get up," she said, standing over him. "The Cleavers are coming, and if you're here when they arrive, you'll get arrested too."

He blinked. "You're letting me go?"

"We're letting *Ryan* go," Skulduggery Pleasant said, walking up behind her. "Ryan was a friend of ours. He deserved better than to be you, Deacon."

"I know he did," Deacon said, rising slowly to his feet for the second time in the last sixty seconds. "I only hope I can make it up to him somehow, maybe by being a better person, by treating people with the same kind of—"

"If you want me to hit you again, you'll keep

talking like that," Valkyrie said.

Deacon shut up. If looks could kill, he'd be skewered. "I know I did wrong," he said, hanging his head. "I know I did. And I've already paid for it. My brother. My poor brother Dafydd. Foe thought Dafydd was me. He chased him and Dafydd... Dafydd fell into that wood chipper. He was always the clumsy one, was Dafydd. So, so clumsy..."

Valkyrie shoved him to get his attention, and when he looked up she leaned in. "If we ever hear of you doing something like that again, creating an innocent person just so you can hide behind them..."

Deacon held up his hands. "I won't, I swear. I've learned my lesson. I was greedy, and selfish. But now I see that it was wrong to—"

"We don't care," Skulduggery said. "Run away before I shoot you."

Deacon nodded, and started walking.

"He said *run*," Valkyrie snarled, and Deacon did just that.

That's NOT all folks!

Read on for an awesome competition, as well as
deleted scenes from the first *Skulduggery Pleasant*
book, chosen and introduced by Derek himself...

DELETED SCENES

When I got the idea for *The End of the World* it was pretty much as it is now. Skulduggery and Valkyrie, seen from a newcomer's perspective, a good kid who develops a crush on our teenage heroine. Tragedy strikes, of course, as tragedy tends to do, punches are thrown, jokes are lobbed, and the sneaky, untrustworthy Deacon runs off at the end, free to get into more misadventures.

I had the idea, I wrote the story. I changed little bits, I edited it, and now it's in your hands. How neat. How tidy. How unusual.

The books aren't like that. The books you read (and hopefully you *will* read them, if you haven't already, because they are by far the best books *ever* written) do not start out the way they finish. I might get done writing the first draft of a book, then completely change it for the second draft. Characters will be switched, some thrown out. Plots will be scrapped, replaced with something new. As much as possible I'll keep scenes and chapters, but I'll just... rearrange them a little.

My original draft of the first book, *Skulduggery Pleasant*, was twice as long as the published version. A lot of what I took out reappears in later books. For example, my original draft had Vengeous and Sanguine and Scapegrace playing important roles, plus a whole new subplot about Stephanie having a vision of her future. On the final page of the original version she learns the truth about her destiny, instead of how it is now, when she learns about it in the fourth book.

How different things would have been if I had kept this in.

There are plenty of deleted scenes I could include here, but most of them would ruin future plot revelations for those who haven't read the books (and you really should, they're really good). So I'm going to concentrate on Valkyrie's home life.

In the books, you see, Valkyrie – or Stephanie, as is her real name – has a reflection that steps out of the mirror and takes over her life. It goes to school, does homework and watches TV with the family while Valkyrie is off saving the world. But in my first draft, there was no reflection, so Valkyrie was always getting into trouble. This led to a major problem, since I wanted her home to be a refuge from conflict, and I wanted her relationship with her folks to be warm and funny and loving. Which is why I came up with the reflection.

But just as a hint of what it could have been like, here are a few excerpts from my original draft.

WHAT MIGHT HAVE BEEN BEEN, PART 1:

(This scene originally stood right before Skulduggery and Stephanie break into the Vault.)

Skulduggery dropped Stephanie off at the entrance to Bayview and promised to contact her the moment he had figured out their next step. The night was drawing steadily in as she approached her house. She slotted her key in the door and twisted and pushed it open, and her mother was standing in the hallway, waiting for her. She wasn't smiling. Her arms were crossed.

"Hi," Stephanie said, closing the door behind her.

"Oh hello," her mother responded. "Enjoy yourself?"

"Sorry?"

"Did you enjoy yourself this evening? Did you have a good time?"

"It was all right," Stephanie said slowly.

"Oh that's good. I'm glad."

Her mother was glaring at her. Stephanie didn't know where to look.

"Is everything OK?" she asked.

"We have visitors."

As she spoke, Fergus and Beryl emerged from the living room. Beryl's hands were clasped in front of her and she had a look of utmost piety on her face. Fergus didn't quite manage to get the look of glee off of his. Stephanie looked back at her mother and waited.

"What were you doing in Mr Pleasant's car?" her mother asked.

Stephanie's thought process came to a sudden stop. Her mother was looking at her, her face angry but her eyes pleading, needing a reasonable explanation. Behind her, Fergus was almost cackling, while Beryl had a false look of deep concern.

"I wasn't—" Stephanie began.

"Yes you were!" barked Fergus immediately. Then, with more control, "We saw you."

"We saw you, dear," Beryl echoed, shaking her head sadly. "We saw you yesterday in that dreadful car of his. It's quite difficult to miss, the way it rattles. And then, just a few short hours ago."

"They came and told me," her mother said. "I had to hear this from Fergus and Beryl."

"We didn't think we had a choice," Beryl trilled. "Stephanie's almost like a daughter to us."

"I got a lift from him," Stephanie said. "So what?"

Her mother looked down. "Don't lie to me, Steph," she said quietly.

"I'm not lying."

"Don't lie to me!" She shouted it this time, her voice filling the hallway.

Stephanie could feel the anger building – not at her mother, but at Fergus and Beryl and their interfering. The only reason they were here was to get back at Stephanie for inheriting Gordon's Estate, she was sure of it.

"Mum…" she started, but once again Fergus cut her off.

"What are you doing with him anyway?" he asked.

"It's none of your business," she snapped.

"We're just looking out for you, dear," Beryl said in that simpering voice of hers.

"Why were you in his car?" her mother asked. "Where did you go this evening? If I don't get answers from you, I'm going straight to Mr Pleasant. I'm going to him anyway, but if you at least try to make me understand..."

"Mum, this isn't a big deal."

Beryl clucked her tongue sadly. "A poor innocent girl, falling in with the wrong crowd..."

Stephanie made a face. "*Wrong crowd?*"

"You don't want to be associated with people like that, dear," Beryl said.

"People like what?"

Beryl had a look of utter distaste as she almost spat the word. "Weirdos."

"This is ridiculous," Stephanie said, her jaw clenching.

"Then how come you won't tell your mother where you've been?" asked Fergus.

"Because it's none of anyone's business!"

Her mother looked at her sternly. "Oh, I think this qualifies as my business. We don't know anything about this Mr Pleasant. We don't know what kind of a man he is."

"And why doesn't he show his face?" Beryl asked, her meddlesome curiosity betraying her serene ambivalence.

"Does he have something wrong with it?" Fergus persisted. "Is it deformed?"

Beryl shivered at the very mention of the word, and

Fergus licked his lips in eagerness. Stephanie wanted to shout at them, to scream at them, but instead she closed herself off and said nothing. She looked at her mother and her mother looked at her.

"Go to your room," her mother said, and Stephanie did so gladly. She didn't even glance at Fergus and Beryl as she climbed the stairs, but when she got to her door she heard Beryl's weed-thin voice saying "It's not her fault, you know. It's the music they listen to..."

WHAT MIGHT HAVE BEEN, PART 2:

(The following scene takes place after Stephanie has been poisoned, and so has been unconscious for over a day.)

Stephanie's eyes suddenly widened. "What time is it?"

"A little past one," Skulduggery said.

"In the morning?" she gasped.

Skulduggery hesitated. "In the next day," he said.

"*What*?"

"You've been unconscious for twenty six hours," China said kindly. "Your parents must be worried sick."

After Stephanie had freaked out, they brought her a phone and stepped out of the room. Stephanie dialled her mother's mobile and held her breath until the call was picked up.

"Steph?" came her mother's frantic voice.

"Hi Mum," she said nervously.

"Oh baby! Where are you? Are you all right?"

"I'm fine, Mum, I'm grand."

"Where are you?" Then, louder; "Desmond! She's OK!" Then, a little less loud; "Where are you?"

"I'm sorry I didn't call."

"What happened to you? We thought something terrible had happened! The police are organising searches and everything!"

Stephanie groaned to herself. "No, Mum, no need to search for me, I'm fine."

"Then what happened?"

She heard her father's voice, demanding to know what's going on, and she heard a short tussle for the phone. Her mother's voice came back to her. "What happened?"

Stephanie swallowed. "I fell asleep."

"You what?"

"I just fell asleep."

"Where are you? Where were you? We called all your friends."

That must have been a quick thirty seconds, Stephanie thought to herself, then, hoping they hadn't checked there; "I was at Gordon's house."

"What were you doing?"

"I just thought I'd look around a little more. I fell asleep on the sofa. I'm really sorry."

There was silence from the other end of the phone.

"Mum?"

"And why didn't you call when you woke up?" Her mother's voice was flat now, devoid of emotion. Stephanie closed her eyes. This was her mother really, really mad.

"I'm calling now."

"It's half one, Stephanie."

"I'm sorry. I must have been really tired."

"Well. Stay where you are, Desmond will be over to pick you up."

"No, I'm not at Gordon's any more, I'm in town. But it's OK, I can get home—"

"You will stay where you are," her mother repeated, "and your father will be over to pick you up. I'd do it myself, but I'm going to be far too busy calling our family and friends, telling them that you're not dead. Oh, and I'll probably tell the police not to bother searching for your body in a ditch somewhere. I'm sure they'd appreciate that."

"OK," Stephanie said meekly.

Fifteen minutes later her father drove up and Stephanie got in the car, acting stronger than she felt. Her father was mad at her too, but it was an obvious kind of mad, and it was tempered by a relief he couldn't hide. As they drove she glanced back and saw China's car in the distance, heading in the opposite direction. Skulduggery had stuck around to make sure she was all right, like she guessed he would.

They got home and Stephanie went to her room and waited for her mother. She sat in her swivel chair, but kept it very still. The door opened, and Stephanie did her best to ignore the fact that the temperature in her bedroom seemed to drop drastically.

"I don't know what's wrong with you lately," her mother said, "I really don't. You're gone all day, you don't get back till late, and all the stories Beryl tells me..."

"Mum, Beryl doesn't like me."

Her mother shook her head. "Don't."

"It's true! Ever since I inherited the Estate they've been out to cause trouble—"

"It's the inheritance, isn't it?"

Stephanie looked up. "What?"

"Your behaviour has been changing ever since you got the inheritance. What, do you think you can play by your own rules now?"

"Mum, no, that isn't it..."

"I think it is. Before this, you barely went out. You barely had any friends. You'd be in your room or you'd be down at the beach, and you'd hardly talk to anyone. We were getting worried about you, actually.

"And now look at you. This Tanith girl, those other people you're hanging around with, the ones that are keeping you out all day. Who are they? I don't know who they are. But they've definitely had an effect on you."

"No they haven't."

"No? You're still the same old Steph?"

"Of course I am."

"The same old Steph wouldn't do the things you're

doing. You've even changed the way you dress, you're wearing those black clothes all the time. We wanted to see you come out of your shell, we've been wanting to see that for a long time, but we didn't expect that the person that came out of that shell would be... would be you."

Stephanie didn't answer. She didn't like this. She didn't like being under constant attack, without the means to fight back. But she couldn't fight back, she couldn't argue, because she didn't know what she might say in her anger. She had to sit here and take it.

"You need to think about what you've done," her mother said. "Think about the people you've hurt, and the people you *are* hurting, and then decide if you think it's worth it."

Her mother left the room, closing the door behind her. Stephanie sat very still, allowed a few moments to slip past, then lashed out, flinging a lamp across the room. It smashed into the wall and dropped.

She blinked, watching as it rolled to a stop on the floor. She hadn't touched it. She'd reached for it and then suddenly it was flying through the air, but she hadn't actually *touched* it. She smiled to herself. Her powers were growing.

Just in time, too.

WHAT MIGHT HAVE BEEN, PART 3:

(The following is a chunk of the original epilogue.)

Valkyrie Cain. She'd taken that name and she'd embraced it, without the slightest idea of what that would entail. She was a part of it now, part of the world that had claimed the life of her uncle, entering into it with gleeful abandon and hideous ignorance. She'd had the audacity to think that because she was descended from the Last of the Ancients, she was somehow meant for this. Meant for magic and marvels and wonders. And what had she seen instead? She'd seen death and destruction, terrors beyond belief and stuff of which nightmares are made.

Silly little girl.

She deserved all the pain she had received. The bruises, the fractures, the cuts, the broken bones? She deserved them, she deserved all of them and more. After all, hadn't she got off lightly? What about poor old Ghastly Bespoke, now nothing more than a ridiculous statue in the back room of his shop? Or Tanith Low, the feisty and brave Tanith Low, skewered by a man who had vanished without a trace? Had Tanith deserved her untimely death? Stephanie was the one who should have died, and she knew it.

Her death would be a release, after all. It would release her parents from having to worry about her. After that night in Haggard, after all the tales of roving gangs and fighting in the streets and Stephanie being at the centre of it all, her poor mother and father were at their wits' end. Her mother hadn't spoken to her in weeks. Her father couldn't even look her in the eye anymore. She hobbled around on her crutches and no one in town wanted to have anything to do with her. She was better off dead.

Even little Jasper was scared of her, little Jasper and his ears that stuck out like car doors. His parents had warned him about her. "*Stay away from that Edgley girl,*" they'd said, "*she's trouble.*" Oh how right they were.

Stay away from that Edgley girl. She's trouble.

It didn't take much to figure out who was really behind all these stories and rumours. Her suspicions were confirmed when she got that phone call.

"Stephanie?"

Yes? she'd said.

"Ah Stephanie, it's Mr Fedgewick here, your late uncle's solicitor."

Oh yes, she'd said. *Do you want to talk to my dad?*

"Actually, I want to talk to you. I felt I had to call, out of a sense of fair play. Your aunt and uncle arrived at my office a few days ago, accompanied by their own solicitor. They requested an examination of the Will. There seems to be a... a possible loophole, in the wording of the document. I am certain your uncle didn't mean it but, nonetheless, it is there."

What's the loophole?

"It seems that you only inherit if you are actually living at home, with your parents, on your eighteenth birthday.

"They were quite insistent that this point be accurate, and they repeatedly proposed the unlikely scenario that if you were not living at home when you turned eighteen, the inheritance would be divided between your parents, and them. I just thought you ought to know."

And that's when it all started to make sense. The constant rumour-mongering, the casting of all those aspersions, planting the seeds of doubt in her parents' minds. They were out to ruin her life, weren't they? Ruin her reputation, ruin her image, and cause rifts between herself and her folks. How wicked. How delightfully Machiavellian in scheme and ambition. They really were to be applauded.

And what could poor old Stephanie do? No one was talking to her, and no one would believe her anyway. She had taken so many trips down to the police station that it was becoming a second home to her. She was notorious, the villain of Haggard. Her crimes grew with each rumour, her sins multiplying with each whisper.

She didn't even have the Bentley to retreat into. Her good and dear friend Skulduggery Pleasant had a lot of cleaning up to oversee. Meritorious had returned and assumed control once more, but his authority was shaky at best. He had, after all, fled at a time when his leadership was needed the most. Around the world, Serpine's allies had resurfaced and struck, and then vanished again when the news of his demise had reached them. Their coup may have failed, but because of it the Cleavers' numbers had been decimated, and their duties stretched them thin. Confidence in the rules and rule-makers was at an all time low. The Sanctuary had been breached, after all. Nothing, and no one, was safe.

Stephanie wasn't involved in these matters, of course. She'd needed time off, time to heal, to mend, and to pretend to be normal. Not that she was fooling anyone. Not any more.

And that was the worst part, wasn't it? She could no longer hope to blend in with the boring and the banal. They knew her now. They knew she was different.

But they still didn't know just how different she was.

———————————

And there you have it – a glimpse of what could have been. Anger and strife instead of warmth and weird jokes. I know which version I prefer.

I hope you found this little insight into the writing process at least vaguely interesting. I had originally wanted to have all these pages blank for you to, like, doodle, or something. But they said no, there had to be stuff. Interesting stuff. With words.

(You can still doodle, though. If you want. In the margins.)

I'm going now. I have work to do. And books to write. And my cat has just sat on my keyboard, and she won't get off.

Derek Landy

WORLD
BOOK
DAY

1 MARCH 2012

Want to **WIN**
a year's supply of **BOOKS**
for you and your school?

Of course you do…

This book is by one of our favourite authors (that's why it's in our **HALL OF FAME**!), but we want to know what *your* favourite book is (or *your* favourite character – whether it's the baddest baddie or the superest hero)!

It's that easy to win, so visit
WWW.WORLDBOOKDAY.COM now!